TRAILER TRAUMA

By Mary Lu Scholl

Trailer Trauma by Mary Lu Scholl

Copyright © 2019 Mary Lu Scholl

All rights reserved.

ISBN: 9781688969490

CONTENTS

Chapter One	1
Chapter Two	7
Chapter Three	23
Chapter Four	29
Chapter Five	35
Chapter Six	51
Chapter Seven	61
Chapter Eight	71
Chapter Nine	85
Chapter Ten	97
Chapter Eleven	107
Chapter Twelve	121
Chapter Thirteen	129
Chapter Fourteen	141
Chapter Fifteen	151
Chapter Sixteen	163
Chapter Seventeen	173
Chapter Eighteen	183
Chapter Nineteen	185

Chapter Twenty	191
Chapter Twenty-one	199
Chapter Twenty-two	209

ACKNOWLEDGEMENTS

There are a great many people who may imagine they see themselves in this work. Not so; I made up characters and imbued them with personalities specifically to fit my stories, myself included. I hope you enjoy them. The park - carefully not named - is a collage of several parks and plopped into Citrus County FL.

Trailer Trauma by Mary Lu Scholl

CHARACTERS

Caroline – Tenant Assoc Secretary

Catherine – Retired Dr of Psychology, Aunt of

Cheyanne – Inscrutable tenant

Dan Brown – A lawyer and baker, Rose Marie's friend

Deputy C Johnson – Baby-faced deputy

Desiree – Park Manager

Detective Dan Boatright – Investigator

Doris – New President tenant association

JJ Jarman – Preacher nephew of Catherine

Marianne – Widow, resident,

Melissa – Miss Mouse – Nathan's girlfriend

Nathan – North neighbor with health issues

Pete – Maintenance man, Doris' boyfriend

Ralph – Affable tenant

Reggie – Indulgent father of Summer

Ronnie – Reluctant Stepmother of Summer

Rose Marie – Not-so-popular resident

Summer – Fading Gospel Singer with a record

TRAILER TRAUMA

CHAPTER ONE

Fall Returns to Central Florida

I debated whether or **not to answer the phone.** **I had saved his number months** ago to my contacts, when he first started calling me. I had never answered or actually even spoken to him.

Nick the Angel responded to my first (and last, and only) foray into online dating. Somehow the idea that he had answered *at all* had been enough to satisfy that itch.

His messages always sounded like an old friend just out of touch for a while. It had actually been some time since he had last called, and I thought he had given up. Somehow the fact that he kept calling imbued him with a sort of desperate air. If he was that desperate he needed someone who would be nice to him. Not me.

That was sufficient salve for *my* conscience, so I ignored his call, again.

I eyed the trailer that had moved into Albert's old space a few days ago.

Trailer, hell, it was a castle on wheels. All it needed was a moat. It even had a drawbridge. Most trailer homes had steps that pulled out. This one's back door had a ramp twice as long as the door was high.

I was predisposed to not like the occupant. Albert had been one of my best friends until he went into the light with my other best friend a few months ago.

Rumor had it this guy was a semi-retired preacher who would save all of us. Of course, other rumors had it that he was a womanizing playboy with a Corvette.

Could be both. After all, this was a Florida Over-55 Mobile Home and RV Park.

The only thing I was reasonably sure of was that he was male. I know women with mustaches and beards, but not like his.

He was vaguely reminiscent of Colonel Saunders.

He even had a cane.

As I stood on my porch drinking my morning smoothie (left over peach pie with peanut-butter powder and vanilla yogurt) I realized he was watching me out of his door. I gulped the last of my diet breakfast.

Great, now I was going to have to make sure I was dressed before coming out on my own porch.

I stormed back inside and slammed the door. It startled Ashes so badly she rolled off the bed from where she had been napping.

She did *not* land on her feet.

"I'm sorry."

Her dignity offended, she hid between the bed and the built-in night-stand.

Maybe if I traded my little truck in for a van my new neighbor wouldn't be able to see over it, and I would have my privacy back...

I liked my truck.

I had a six foot solid board fence around two sides of my porch. The third side was my twenty-five foot travel trailer. It was filled with plants, half-covered by a vendor tent, and open to the short side where I parked. Perfect for a hermit who wanted to *live* on her porch.

A twenty-five foot trailer, what *was* I thinking?

Maybe a clothesline would block his view and give me my privacy back.

Tacky.

CHAPTER TWO

The Castle Inhabitants

"Hey, did you see the sign in the back window of his trailer?" Rose Marie and I sipped root beer kool-aid out of my re-purposed pickle jars and contemplated my new neighbor. "It looks like an open hand with a heart and a ball of some kind."

I narrowed my eyes. "Questions Answered" was written across the top.

"Colonel Saunders is a psychic? That's an interesting twist to the retired-preacher-themed rumor."

Rose Marie offered a different explanation. "Doesn't the church claim to give you answers?"

Colonel Saunders had just left in his classic gold Sebring convertible; it wasn't a Corvette, but it was close.

Suddenly a window opened in the back of the trailer, the room with the ramp, and we could hear the television come on.

"There's someone else in there! Have you heard anything about a wife?" Rose asked me, eyes narrowing.

"Not a peep."

"Let's take over the cookies I brought you. I'll give you more, later."

"What makes you think it's a woman?" I gave a querulous answer because visiting strangers was not on my 'pleasant ways to spend an afternoon' list.

"Let's go see."

I scared up a piece of my everyday china (a paper plate with red white and blue stars) and we set off across the rip-rap driveway. I stood to one side of the ramp as Rose Marie stepped up and knocked. The television was switched off, or at least put on mute.

"Come in - it's not locked."

Twisting the knob and pulling out on the door, Rose reached a hand to help pull me up and I followed her into a surprisingly roomy space.

There was a twin size bed against the wall with cabinets above it, drawers beneath. A couch faced the bed, with a small built-in table on the wall between them. A flat screen TV, turned off, hung from the ceiling overhead. On the table, behind a candle and a Kindle, was a crystal ball with a swirled blue center.

I was staring at the room while Rose Marie - who always had better manners than I - introduced us to a little woman perched at the head of the bed, bolstered by stacked pillows and a quilt behind her.

"I'm Rose Marie and this is Patty." She nudged my elbow so I would pay attention. "Patty lives next door to you and I live on the other side of the park."

The woman had a halo of curly gray hair with very large, very round glasses. Even with the tiny bifocal lines they made her look like an owl. Her clothing was barn-owl-brown, but was velour instead of feathers.

I checked with my tongue to see if I had remembered to put my top teeth in. Without them, I lisp and look like an overripe jack-o-lantern. With them, I am socially acceptable.

Thank goodness I was appropriately dentured. I reached over to shake hands. "Welcome to the 'hood."

She narrowed her eyes at me, heavy eyebrows forming a deep V. Whatever she was deciding, her response took the form of propriety. "I'm sure."

"I'm Catherine, nice to meet you." She turned a warm smile onto Rose Marie. Rose was friendly and attractive; she was rounded in a comfortable way and she dressed to suit it with pretty floral dresses and a nice smile. It was natural for strangers to like her on sight.

Besides, she was carrying cookies.

I was lumpier and my natural expression was one of doubt and suspicion. Rose Marie claims I am improving, though.

"Please, sit down ladies. How nice! Can I get you something to drink to go with those cookies?"

Rose hesitated. "Water would be perfect. I'm closer to the kitchen, would you like me to get it?" It was Catherine's room that had the ramp outside, so Rose wasn't sure if she was mobility challenged or if the ramp was just a coincidence. Because Rose Marie was naturally thoughtful, she offered to fetch.

"It might be easier at that. I just drink water during the day, as well. That's a pocket door, just slide it to the left and go through the bathroom."

Catherine turned her attention to me as Rose busied herself in her natural habitat - the kitchen. "Have you met my nephew?"

Well, that clarified that relationship. "Not really, I have seen him a couple of times, but we haven't done more than nod."

Actually, he had nodded and I had ignored him.

"He looks like a very nice man. I've heard he's a retired preacher, is that right?"

"If you mean between churches, yes, he's retired. I hope he finds a new flock before he drives me crazy."

I couldn't help it, I giggled.

She smiled.

This might work; we might be able to share the cul-de-sac amiably.

"Are you a psychic?" Rose Marie asked as she returned with three insulated plastic glasses. They were individually decorated with sea horses on one, a manatee on another, and palm trees on the third.

Catherine reached for the palm trees and answered "No."

Rose Marie and I exchanged glances. "Somehow, I can't see a preacher hanging out that shingle in your window." I prompted.

"You two are obviously friends. So you have each other to talk to. You both seem to have self-confidence; there's nothing reticent about either of you. You're also the first people to come see me," she took a bite of cookie, "even if you did wait until my nephew left."

I interrupted. "We didn't know you were here until you opened the window and turned the television on."

"No need to get defensive, I was just explaining you don't fit my target demographic."

She continued as Rose swept her skirt under her and settled next to me on the sofa.

"I get really, really bored. I'm Doctor Catherine, a retired psychologist. I never actually tell anyone I'm a psychic. I just put on a headscarf, and turn the lights down. I tell people things they want or need to hear."

I was appalled. "Fraud comes to mind."

She laughed at me. "The sign says "questions answered." Does it give any other promise?"

Rose Marie looked disapproving as well.

"Come on, you two. Give me the benefit of the doubt. Answering questions was what I did for forty years and charged good money for."

"You don't charge, now?" I asked.

"No. I just like to help, and I like company. I can walk, but not far or for very long. This way people come to me."

Rose smiled at that one.

"Also," Catherine continued, "I feel obligated to make people happy when they are paying me. If I don't charge them, I'm free to tell them what I think, and they're free not to come back."

She took another, bigger, bite of one of the Snickerdoodles. "Oh my! This is wonderful! Which of you is the baker?"

"Definitely Rose Marie," I told her as my friend blushed.

"I can see I'll either have to limit my access to you two, or devise some sort of exercise." She devoured another one.

"There's an exercise room with stationary bicycles, a rower and other things you might be able to use," I volunteered.

I had no idea if any of them worked.

"Also a pool. Right now, though, you have to swim around all the floaties during the day. There's a swim-only time set by the tenant association, but it's ridiculously early in the morning. Maybe you would like to come to the next meeting."

Catherine considered the idea. She, unlike Rose, was not shocked by the unusual length of my speech. "Maybe I will. Let me know when and where."

"She's quite a character," Rose commented as we returned to our respective homes. "I think I like her."

"I wonder about her nephew." I was considering the difficulty of being friends with the aunt when I had already decided I didn't like the nephew.

Rose Marie knew me all too well.

"Honestly, Patty. You haven't even met him. How can you have decided already that he's a cad or a scoundrel in just a week?" She turned back to face me before she headed across the common area.

"Come with, and I'll get you some more cookies."

Forsaking dignity in favor of cinnamon, I trotted after her. Her side of the park was mostly full-time residents, all in single or double mobile homes, and I didn't spend much time over there. I referred to it as "the dark side" most of the time. In general, the full-timers and even some of the snowbirds, tended to look just a little down on the mostly temporary tenants on my side.

I fell sort of in the middle. I lived in an RV, but lived there year around, so they didn't know what to make of me.

Which was fine. I wasn't exactly social to start with. I only moved down here after my fourth husband died, to be close to my son. He was promptly transferred back up north.

"Nothing personal, Mom."

Right. He actually did ask if I wanted to go with him, back up to snow country.

Nope. I chose warmth.

CHAPTER THREE

More Neighbors, What's The 'Hood Coming To?

"Hey Rose," I called back over my shoulder as I left with my new bag of calories, "someone's moving into the Bird House."

There was a box truck backed into the driveway of the green mobile home at the entrance of my cul-de-sac. It had been empty for a while, ever since Jessica was taken away.

Rose's voice floated out the door as she spread pretty waxed material over the remaining cookies, to give later to some client or another.

"Hold on a minute while I start the hotpot - I'm fixing Harold a roast. We'll go meet them."

Harold was one of her clients. Rose Marie made ends meet by performing wifely duties for those guys who couldn't do things themselves- or preferred not to. For Harold, she shopped and cooked dinner a couple of times a week on his tab and split the leftovers with him. For Daniel, she fixed a big breakfast on Friday morning and did his laundry. He paid her electric bill.

A lot of women in the park were catty about it, speculating on what other services might be offered, but Rose ignored them. She and I agreed they considered her to be competition to their marriage plans and were just jealous.

We stepped around the new neighbors' truck and I knocked lightly on the door frame as Rose Marie called out a greeting. Normally we would have just called out and gone in, but these were new folks and may not have been receptive to our informality.

An older woman with spikey gray hair and wire-rimmed glasses answered with a soft southern accent. "Come in; good afternoon." She put down a small box and turned toward us.

"I'm Rose Marie and this is Patty. I live just around the corner, and Patty actually lives only a few yards down the driveway next to you."

"I'm Veronica and my husband is Reginald. Ronnie and Reggie, of course, for short. My step-daughter will live here as well. Summer." She smoothed her apron down - not a cooking apron, but one with pockets for things like pliers. "I'd offer you a cup of tea and cookies, but..." and she gestured at the stacked boxes and little else that surrounded her so far. I couldn't help it, I was sure I heard a snide undertone.

"Welcome here," Rose offered, "we just stopped by to be nosy and welcome you." She and I turned to go back out the door and Ronnie followed us. "Will you be here year-around or are you going to be snowbirds?" Rose continued.

"We haven't completely decided just how much time we'll spend here. We have another home in Fort Myers and another one outside Nashville." Reggie had joined the conversation.

Did I see Ronnie glare at him? What the heck for?

"Music people?" Rose Marie asked Reggie hopefully as we stepped off the porch.

"Kind of. Summer is a gospel singer. We'll have to have a party and invite everyone over when we get unpacked." Ronnie took over the conversation. Then she turned at the door, disappearing without another word and ending the visit abruptly.

I looked at Rose Marie. "Is that what you call a bum's rush?"

CHAPTER FOUR

Tenant Association Meeting

The clubhouse, like the park, was beginning to fill up again. Fall brought the snowbirds down and the park was busy with people pulling in, opening the shutters over their windows, renewing acquaintance with each other, and with those of us who actually live here in paradise year-around.

I eyed the people scattered around the room in anticipation of the meeting. Rose Marie wouldn't be there. She was so often the target of their 'resolutions' that she had stopped coming long ago. Doris, the relatively new President of the Association, was seated at the front of the room with Caroline, her secretary, at her side.

Pete, her boyfriend and our maintenance man, was protectively in the front row close to the door. A big man, good looking, he nodded at me but didn't speak. We had sort of a stand-off going on since I had sent his previous girlfriend to prison, but then stuck up for him in a later case.

The number of people attending the meetings had increased after the last president went to jail. She had been just a tad-bit overbearing, and had run a lot of people off from participating.

I hadn't filed assault charges. I should have.

Marianne had not come. Nor had Nathan (my north neighbor) or his girlfriend, Miss-Mouse. (What was her real name?) I had started calling her Miss-Mouse in my head, because of her appearance, and simply could *not* remember her name. This was often a source of subtle friction with Nathan, who for some reason considered it rude that I couldn't remember her name. If he had any idea how long it had taken me to remember *his* name...

I realized I had forgotten to tell Castle-dweller Catherine that the meeting was tonight. (Now why did I remember *her* name?)

Neither Ronnie nor Reggie came, but that didn't really surprise me.

A hush fell over the predominantly female room and I looked toward the door. Colonel Saunders entered the room, his elegant cane hooked over one wrist.

He nodded politely to Pete and swept his hat off with a slight bow to Doris. She blushed just a little. It was a good thing Pete was looking at him instead of her. The Colonel settled into a seat next to him, with an air of comradery.

"My aunt couldn't make it tonight," he confessed to Pete.

Murmurs started up around the room and Doris banged her gavel - yes, really - a gavel.

"This meeting will come to order. Caroline, will you please review the last meeting for us?"

Caroline cleared her throat and shuffled the paper in front of her. "There were rumors that the park was going to be sold." She looked to Doris.

"Yes. The Park has been sold. The closing is scheduled for next week."

Voices all clashed with each other until Doris banged her gavel again.

"Caroline, please continue with the review. Further discussion on this topic will be held afterward."

Caroline spoke again; Doris' authority bolstering her confidence. "There was discussion about the large hole behind space 24 and whether or not it was a sink hole. Speeding on the old road east of us was mentioned. Removal of the owl nesting by the retention pond was discussed because she represents a hazard to our cats and smaller dogs. The cultivation of non-native and possibly invasive plants was brought up. Several of the chairs around the pool need to be either re-painted or replaced."

Doris stood up with effort. She had serious edema in her legs that limited her standing time, but she thought that it was important to stand up at this point in each meeting. "The hole behind space 24 was not a sinkhole; Brad removed a tree with the manager's permission. It's been filled in."

"We have no control over roads outside the park, but concern over speeding has been shared with the Sheriff's Office."

"The owls are gone."

"I refuse to address any more petty concerns regarding Rose Marie, her cats, her bees, or her garden. Get over it. Her flowers are an asset to the community." She glared at the frowning women in the back of the room.

"The faded chairs will have to be addressed with the new owners of the park unless you want to have a fund-raiser and have the tenant association spend the money."

She waited for someone to agree or disagree.

The previous president had ruled the park with an iron fist; this benefitted Doris because the tenants were not accustomed to questioning their ruler.

"Okay. The park has tentatively been sold to an out-of-state corporation that owns a number of other Over-55 parks around the country, and a couple more here in Florida. It's called Parks Unlimited. Other than that, I know only what you can find on the internet. If you have questions, we will compile them and I'll go to Desiree for answers, for the next meeting. Are you ready, Caroline?"

"Are they going to change the name of the park?" A woman up front asked.

"If they change the name of the park, will we have to change our addresses?" A man in the middle. "Will we get a new mailman?"

"Are they going to raise the rent? I heard they always double the rent." A voice quavered in the back. "I'll have to move."

"Will they dig up the shuffleboard and horseshoe areas to make more spaces?" I recognized that voice; Howard had run for president, and lost to Doris.

"Are they going to keep Desiree?"

"I think SOME of us have too many flamingos and lights in their yard - it's tacky."

"Are they going to keep Pete?"

"Are they going to dissolve the tenant association?"

"What about feral cats? Are they going to crack down on feral cats? How about dogs? Are big dogs going to be outlawed? I don't think snakes should be allowed."

"Did you get all that?" Doris asked Caroline when there was a lull in the questions.

Another voice spoke with authority. "They need to pave the south road, or at least grade it again and put down rip-rap or something." Several voices murmured in agreement; the ruts there were beyond treacherous. "Also, there have been three more instances of firecrackers going off under people's golf carts in the middle of the night. Why hasn't the Sheriff's Department found who is responsible?"

There was a chorus of agreement.

"Tell them they should get rid of all the trailers and motorhomes and move more mobile homes in." A woman in a pastel pink polyester pantsuit proposed. "No offense," she said to me.

Doris raised her hand for quiet. "I'll be sure to ask how many flamingos represent excessive lawn ornamentation." I wasn't sure, but I thought I saw her roll her eyes just slightly.

"Obviously, the new owner is not going to invest in the park at this moment. It won't be theirs for several more days. Nor is the old owner interested in changes or non-essential upkeep at this point. Nor can I expect an immediate answer to maintenance schedules or improvements by the new owner. We need to wait until after Parks Unlimited actually takes over and is ready to talk to me."

"Please add the road thing to the list, however." Doris offered as an aside to

Caroline, "and the firecrackers; I would like to know who is scaring the fingerprints off people, too."

"If anyone has any idea who is doing it, call the Sheriff's Office, please." This, to the audience at large.

"When's the next meeting? Do you really think we can wait that long for answers?" I admit it. That was me; the one who didn't really care, just wanted to stir stuff up.

"Thank you, Patty."

Was there a hint of sarcasm there?

"I'll post a report of the answers on the usual bulletin boards as soon as I get one typed. I'll send it to anyone who has already given me an e:mail address."

"Good luck with that."

I didn't know who said that, but he was right. I could hardly do anything on the internet in the park. I was lucky if I got two bars when I accessed my publishing website. Look under 'abysmal' in the dictionary for more information.

"We should change the 'swimming only' time at the pool. "It's ridiculous."

That was me, too. I don't swim. I just cause trouble and solve murders, and we hadn't had a murder in months. I was bored.

"We'll see what we can do." Doris gestured to Caroline to add my suggestion, and again rolled her eyes at me because she *knew* I didn't swim.

"Is there any other new business?"

Colonel Saunders stood up. "JJ Jarman here. My lady aunt and I have just moved into space 23. I have retired from the pulpit of a verra demanding church farther south, but I find my calling didna retire with me."

"I understand that presently this fine community depends on a televised sermon, every Sunday, here in this *very* room." He gestured in a stately manner with his hat, somehow relaying that he found the room impressive.

"I would like to offer my services, should you decide to accept them, to provide divine guidance at some time on Sunday that does not conflict with my colleague on the television. I am sure you derive great benefit from her leadership and insight, but there is nothing like being able to just open up your heart and receive blessings in person, through a humble man of God."

Colonel JJ grasped his hat brim with both hands and held it modestly in front of him, head bowed. When someone started to speak, JJ raised his hand, palm outward, and there was instant silence.

"You needn't decide, or commit, right now; not without prayer for guidance. Go home, search your heart, and pray. With permission from Miss Doris and Miss Desiree, I will be here ...at noon... on Sunday... to worship on my own, and you are welcome to join me."

He lowered his hand and raised his head and the crowd started clapping.

I was amazed. Even Quinn, Marianne's late roommate, who had run for association president before Doris, had not commanded a room that well.

There was relative silence when Doris dismissed the meeting and we poured out into the sultry, starry, night, and headed home. As I detoured past Howard's home, for no real reason, an explosion of firecrackers erupted from under his golf cart.

I nearly had a heart attack. Served me right for taking the long way. This was the newest plague in the park. No one seemed to know who was setting them off, apparently with a ridiculously long fuse (said the deputies who hadn't caught him yet).

By the time I got my breath back, lights were coming on in the homes of the neighbors. I just went home, I hadn't seen anyone and would have nothing to add to any official report.

CHAPTER FIVE

...Helps Those Who Help Themselves...

It was a good thing televangelist Martha was unaware of the number of watchers who abandoned her on Sunday morning to come listen to JJ Jarman an hour later. It would have hurt her feelings. I sat on the veranda of the building, in one of the faded chairs, with my laptop open, just to see who came.

I was nosy; so sue me.

I could see Dahlia, the little ghost girl, swinging on her oak tree swing. Even after two years she still wouldn't talk to me, but she did nod.

Catherine wasn't there for her nephew's inaugural message. I really wondered about that...

JJ was very good. I couldn't even fault any of his message, and usually *something* irritated me.

His message was about charity of the heart. He used dramatic gestures and even used the blackboard at one end of the room. In big block letters it said:

LOVE EVERYONE, I'LL SORT THEM OUT LATER. GOD

I hated to admit it, but he might not be so bad for such a smoothie. He didn't even pass a collection plate for a love offering.

Caroline sidled up to him after the message and invited him, and his aunt, to her house for an early dinner. I saw him nod and give her a safe one-armed hug.

Interestingly, Dahlia was at the window. That was the first time I had ever seen her leave her yard.

Harley Davidson Rex was there, sitting by Pete and Doris. He didn't hang around, just took off on the motorcycle he had ridden all of 50 yards to the clubhouse.

Mary Lu Scholl

CHAPTER SIX

Sirens, both kinds

I had just opened up a new manuscript and set up the template for a new book. Then I stared at it.

The phone rang. It was my son Nick. That was a good excuse to push the laptop away.

"What's up, Son? You usually text me." That was superfluous, he would know that. "Is something wrong? Are you getting married yet?"

He laughed. "You're invited, Mom. She's fifty and has three children, all teenagers. It might be a while because I have to convert to her religion first."

"It's a good thing you have the same sense of humor I do. If I didn't know you so well, you'd give me a heart attack."

"Not you, Mom. You're healthy as the proverbial horse. I'm just checking in. What's new on the Nature Coast of Paradise?"

"I've moved the travel trailer to a nudist colony to save on laundry."

"That's nice; send pictures."

"How's work?"

"What doesn't kill you makes you stronger."

"You should try on-line speed-dating."

"That's two different things. Also, I don't think anyone does speed-dating anymore. That's what Facebook is for."

"I'm going to be too old for grandchildren, soon!"

Sirens rent the background of the park.

"What's that noise?"

"Probably just a low-flying airplane, taking pictures. Talk to you later, I'm glad you called." I hit 'end' on my phone. No reason to upset the boy.

I stuck my head out the door to see if the sirens were coming into the park.

I saw them coming up the dark side. I grabbed my sandals and headed out the door.

I went back for my teeth.

While I was back inside, the cruiser pulled right across the driveway that leads to my cul-de-sac. An ambulance pulled up behind it.

As soon as the sirens stopped, I could hear loud voices coming from the trailer Ronnie and Reggie moved into. The big screen porch that wrapped two sides of the trailer did nothing to stop the sound, but the dark mesh blurred sight of what was going on, at least until a fist poked right through it.

The deputy shouted at someone to stop and slammed open the porch door. The other voices stopped. Then a flower pot went clean through the screen and smashed on the driveway. I heard scuffling again.

I decided this was a good time to take out my trash. It's one hundred three steps to the trash dumpster, fortunately right past the action. I ducked inside for the plastic sack and headed off.

"Be good, Ashes. Mom will be right back." She didn't care, just blinked.

The two EMTs were sitting on their bumper, waiting for Deputy Charlie to tell them it was safe.

The deputy had started another mustache. Without it, he looked about fourteen. With it, he looked about fourteen-and-a-half with a dirty face. I'd already told him that, and he'd ignored me with all the southern civility his mama had managed to switch into him.

He was helping a woman to her feet. Her hands were bound behind her with a zip-tie. Long blonde hair was tangled around her face, and one sleeve of her blouse was torn. They staggered down the steps together and across the driveway. He put one hand on the top of her head to protect it while he crowded her into the back seat of his unit.

I had reached the end of the rip-rap drive and paused to watch; that *was* why I was there, after all.

I was a writer; that was my excuse for most of the questionable things I did. Hopefully the FBI would never go through my browser history.

"Miss Patty, please stand back and let the EMTs come ahead onto the porch."

By that time I was no longer alone. Half-a-dozen people with nothing better to do were standing around. I just wanted to know who got hurt and how badly. The woman in the Sheriff's vehicle must have laid down across the seat, we couldn't see her.

I stood there, trash in hand but forgotten. People started whispering and one was evidently elected to talk to me; not something people do lightly. Where *did* they get the idea that I knew everything that was going on?

"Miss Patty, do you know what happened?"

"I believe she's being arrested for smuggling."

Miss Mouse was horrified and believed every word of it. She scurried away. I sighed. Next time, she wouldn't believe anything I said.

I saw the EMT's bandaging Ronnie's head. I heard Reggie's deep voice. He was trying to make excuses for someone. That was all I needed to know. I knew Deputy Charlie wasn't going to tell me anything else. His boss, Detective Danny Boatright, made sure Charlie knew to keep me at a distance so I couldn't weasel stuff out of him.

Having sown the seeds of gossip, I headed back to my place. I tossed the trash sack into the back of my truck to drop off later.

Mary Lu Scholl

CHAPTER SEVEN

Eggs with catsup and gossip

I was scrambling eggs with peppers, onion, sausage, and cheese for a late lunch.

There was a loud rapping on my metal door. I picked up my remote and put pause on the Duke as he shot up a whole gang of outlaws. I flung my door open in irritation.

Catherine stood there, supported by a light-weight walker. It was unencumbered with all the holders and accoutrements you usually see, just a basic get-you-to-your-neighbor's-porch model. Catherine had shed her velour for blue cotton shorts and a long sleeve T-shirt. To each her own.

Her face was even grumpier than mine. Refreshing!

"Hi. What's up?"

"Are you coming out here or do I have to figure out how to get up your steps?"

"I have scrambled eggs, enough for two; want some lunch, or dinner, or whatever you want to call it?"

She eyed me warily. "Do you have catsup?"

"Sure. Sit down anywhere. I'll be out in a minute."

Unaccountably, my mood was lightened and I stepped out with two paper plates of eggs, a bottle of catsup and another of hot sauce.

"What brings you over?"

"You have let me down as a neighbor and I wanted to hold you accountable."

I blinked.

"Not only did you not come to get me for the Tenant Association Meeting, but you haven't shared any sort of gossip about the sirens."

"On top of that, you haven't tried to warn me about the predatory females who are circling my nephew like sharks."

She took a big bite of eggs while I recovered from shock.

"I don't know where you get off expecting so much out of me. Wasn't it clear when we met that I'm not exactly what you would call social?" I took a bite as well. "Would you like more salt and pepper?" I asked, only because I did.

"Yes, thank you. I know you're not; but I don't know which mobile home is Rose's so I decided to take it out on you. Besides, you're close enough for me to get to."

I brought the salt and pepper out and handed it to her.

"That makes sense." It did. "I forgot about getting you for the meeting; but your nephew came! Why didn't you come with him?"

"I get extremely sleepy when he doesn't want me along. Sometimes I catch him with the sleeping pills, sometimes I don't. That time I didn't."

I gaped. She shrugged; as if getting drugged was a normal thing.

"The sirens were a domestic dispute between our neighbor's grown daughter and her stepmother. Can't say for sure, but alcohol was probably involved - on the daughter's side."

Her eyes grew wide. "What happened?"

"She's still in jail, I think. I told someone she was a smuggler, so if you hear that story, just nod and forget it."

"My turn. Who is sniffing around JJ?" I was dying of curiosity.

She snorted. "Go by the pool some morning when he swims. Who isn't?"

"Me. Rose. Doris. Carlotta. Marianne." Naturally I took her question literally.

She had to backtrack to realize she had asked a question. "Point taken. There's one named Caroline? There's another one, I think her name is Betty. Actually, I think there *was* a Marianne in there somewhere. Oh, and another one he's being secretive about."

"Summer, a singer?"

She looked surprised; she blinked and was quiet for a minute.

I elucidated. "She's the one in jail. What's his level of interest in a relationship and why do you care?"

She polished off her plate. "He might be difficult sometimes, but we get along pretty well. I like having him around for company, errands, etcetera. He hates it that he isn't with a church right now, or, hates not getting paid, anyway. I keep him on a short financial leash because he has demonstrated a lack of common sense when it comes to money."

She sat back and folded her hands in her lap.

"He plays around, and he honestly does like women and their company, but he prefers the ones who have money to spend on him and his 'causes'. If he finds a rich one to marry, I might have to find a new driver."

"Maybe a new one wouldn't drug you." That whole idea just appalled me. "In that case, let it slip that Betty is broke, living on social security, and eats from the various free pantries around the county."

"Caroline may be a good match for him, if he likes animals," I added.

"Animals?"

"Two dogs, two cats, two gerbils, two birds, two hedgehogs, and two snakes. You may infer from the list that the park limits pets to two of a species."

"So did Noah. I can pretty much guarantee he won't be moving in with her, he hates snakes. She won't be moving in with us, either. Even if she leaves them all at her house. Two is plenty in my trailer. But if they just want to play together for a while, she might work."

"If he thrives on drama, though, Marianne or Summer might interest him."

Catherine scraped the last morsel off her plate and stood up abruptly. "Glad we had this little talk. Drop by my place next time." She stood, a little wobbly, and headed home to her castle.

"Thanks for dinner," she called back, "my doctor disapproves of eggs so I don't get them much."

I stood to take things in. "I disapprove of your doctor!" I called after her.

CHAPTER EIGHT

Being Neighborly

Mindful of my neighborly duties, I walked thirty steps and knocked on Catherine's door. I had in hand the posted responses to the questions regarding the purchase of the park. I had taken it down from the clubhouse door immediately after Doris hung it up. She hadn't left yet, so she hung another one up. "You could have just asked for a copy, you know."

"And ruin my reputation by being polite?"

She guffawed, and her omnipresent guardian, Pete, shook his head at me. "I think you're all talk; just an old softie," he said.

"Who are you calling old?"

He glared at my tone of voice and we were back to our stand-off.

I waited until I saw JJ pull out of the park. He had a woman with him, but then, he usually did. This one was blonde but at that distance I couldn't really see her.

Catherine yelled that it was unlocked, so I just opened it and went in.

"No cookies?" She asked.

"No cookies, just news. Why? Do you have cookies?"

"No. But I have banana bread and cream cheese."

"I'll get it. Here, read this," I headed for her kitchen.

She was done reading it by the time I returned with our snack.

"Any surprises? This is the first park I ever lived in, so I don't know what usually goes on when one gets sold." Catherine reached for her piece of banana bread and I picked up the paper again.

"It doesn't look like a lot of changes, at least not the ones we asked about." I scanned down the list of specific questions again. "Yes to the new name. No, to the new addresses. That was a stupid question anyway. The new name makes sense. If we're going to belong to a chain, they'll want people to recognize it by the name."

"They don't anticipate major changes to the park rules. *People and Programs*, I suppose that means the Tenant Association, Pete and Desiree, *will remain in place for the foreseeable future*."

"*Changes will include lighting at the highway entrance, a security gate, new signs, and all roads to be re-paved or improved. Furniture in and around common areas to be replaced, benches, tables and chairs*."

Catherine had already lost interest in the sale of the park. "Did you know Betty also has a thing for Pete, as well as JJ?"

I looked at her in amazement.

"Don't look so surprised. She came to have her fortune told. I mentioned an elusive man in her life - which is normally a good bet - and she volunteered the name Pete. Then she told me he lived here and not to say anything to him. Has to be the maintenance guy. She didn't say anything about not telling JJ, so he must know she's interested."

"She's a couple of bases shy of a home run." The absurdity of Pete and Betty didn't even leave me room for an answer. She was old enough to be his mother, and he was no spring chicken. Plus, he was devoted to Doris. I just stared a minute and went back to the notes.

"It also says they're placing a bid on the property next door that the previous manager, Jeremiah, has for sale."

Catherine took a bite out of her bread. "The Bimbo is home from jail. JJ just left, and I think he was taking her to lunch. I overheard the phone call. She invited him, but he wasn't exactly dragging his heels."

"I haven't actually seen her clearly. Being dragged across the driveway doesn't count. What does she look like?"

"She looks about fifty something. Dresses well. Bottle blonde. Too much make-up. Typical lead-singer who doesn't actually play anything. She didn't come in, I looked out the window."

I finished my last bite and realized I didn't bring napkins. I licked my fingers and wiped my hands on my shorts when I stood up to leave. "You don't know who is setting off firecrackers, do you?" I wondered if Catherine could become a source of information.

"Is *that* what that was last night?"

"Your turn; next time anything comes up." I called back as I shut the door. I heard a muffled laugh and grinned.

What was it with the phone lately? I was really spoiled by Albert, who as a ghost, just popped in and out and told me what was going on and when. No one ever used to call me. I detest being summoned in the middle of a pleasant afternoon by a plastic device; or anytime, come to think of it.

It was Marianne. "Patty, can you come over?"

A pretty woman, very 'northern'. She had moved down here with her friend, Quinn, after they both lost their spouses. They were just roommates, but had been close friends for a long time. She was devastated when he was murdered not long ago. She had been wearing dark colors ever since.

I was cutting through the horseshoe pits when I saw a strange woman smoking a cigarette under one of the big oak trees. I stopped because she was blonde - unusual in a gray-haired community. A pick-up truck pulled up and stopped. She threw her cigarette on to the ground and waited for the man. He stalked toward her. She backed up a little. He raised one hand and pointed his finger at her as he started to speak.

He saw me looking at them and nodded in my direction. She turned for a second and I got an impression of a sly smile. He grabbed her arm and opened his passenger door. She climbed in willingly, and he sped away before I could get all the way across.

"Come in!" Marianne called automatically as I opened the door. Rose Marie was right behind me.

"Hi, Ladies. Tea? Wine? Lemonade?"

We settled at her table, expectantly, as she poured the requests.

"I'm going to have a little barbeque. I hope you'll come. Rose, you have the tightest schedule, what day would be best for you and Dan?"

Rose fingered her glass and hesitated. "I'll have to talk to Dan and let you know." Her eyes were focused on her fingers and she didn't elaborate.

"Patty? Any commitments?"

"You're serious? Since when?" I was suspicious, though. "Since when do you entertain? You haven't had anyone over in...forever."

Having said that, I noticed she was wearing a pink dress. Her hair was perfect, as usual. Was her lipstick a shade lighter?

"I thought I'd invite our new preacher and his aunt. It would be a nice way to welcome them and help them get to know everyone."

Pink dress; this all had to do with Colonel Saunders, I'd bet. JJ, I corrected myself. "I'll do beans."

"I'll make cornbread, if you'd like. Who else is coming?" Rose Marie volunteered.

"I'll wait until you let me know what evening is best, then I'll invite Doris, Pete, you know, an assortment."

"Just pick a day. Dan may not be able to come; he's been working a lot, lately. How about next Thursday?"

"Rose, did I tell you Doris told the biddies in the park to lay off you? At the last meeting, she even said your flowers are an asset."

She smiled at that. Something was wrong. She should have laughed.

I couldn't resist the temptation to throw a wrinkle into Marianne's plans. "You ought to invite Ronnie and Reggie, as well, and their daughter." I gave my best innocent look. "They're new, too."

Marianne looked at me suspiciously - just to see if I was trying to cause trouble.

Me?

"I'll have to consider that," she responded carefully.

"There's that other newish guy, too. One that rides a motorcycle. Sexy Rexy."

Rose looked at me, aghast that such an appellation would even occur to me. "Seriously, Patty?"

Marianne had stopped listening to us. No doubt she thought she was being crafty in her plan to capture JJ's attention.

Marianne was a very nice woman, but, with all my love and respect, not especially smart.

CHAPTER NINE

Subtlety

I couldn't help it, I had to laugh. It was a good thing I was behind the scenes, helping in the kitchen when JJ walked in with his '+ one'.

Marianne had completely lost control of the guest list. She had carefully invited about 15 people. She sent out the original invitations as post cards delivered to their porches and added '+ one' to the single people, so she expected twenty-five or so.

Rose bustled in with all the sausages and hamburgers she had in her freezer. I had stockpiled baked beans when they were on sale recently and had already fetched more of them. Marianne's larder was already decimated.

"It's a good thing you made a ton of cornbread," I told Rose. "I have some hot dogs. I can chop them into bites and put them in the slow cooker, with catsup and grape jelly. We're out of real barbeque sauce."

"Go get them." Rose Marie wiped the hair off her forehead as soon as she had a hand free. It was sweltering in the kitchen.

"At least we have warm weather!" Marianne said as she came into the kitchen after more deviled eggs.

As I hurried past, I saw JJ with Caroline on his arm. He had interpreted '+ one' as a date, separate from his aunt, who was already ensconced on the porch. To her credit, Marianne carried on as hostess and welcomed him, *and* his less welcome date, on the heels of Ronnie and Reggie.

Why should I feel guilty? I didn't help Marianne with her invitations, wording, etcetera, nor did I anticipate the circus she started.

Rose Marie's Dan had not come, so Marianne had asked Pete to help 'man the meat' as the she put it.

A dark Range Rover pulled up in front of the clubhouse, kitty-corner from Marianne's. It was notable because no one in the park had one; and because it was new, bright, and shiny.

The passenger door opened and a pair of legs slid out. The body followed the legs and the blonde head came last as she seemed to float to the ground. She turned back quickly to wiggle her fingers at the other occupant, wiggle her skirt down to a modest level, and slam the door.

I finally saw Summer clearly, and she was just like Catherine had described her. *A Streetcar Named Desire* came to mind. She was remarkably unaffected by the whispers around her. Maybe she didn't remember being carried out in a squad car. Maybe it was so common in her world as to be unremarkable. Obviously unrepentant.

"Maybe you should ask Colonel Saunders if he would mind helping Pete," I suggested. Marianne looked blank. She was totally focused on the newcomer.

"It would get him away from Caroline, and I'm sure Pete would appreciate it." I explained patiently.

I could see her brow furrow. "Colonel...oh! You mean JJ!."

"You're devious," Rose shook her head later. "Are you sure Marianne and JJ would be a good thing? Men can be iffy at best."

I resisted mentioning Dan's absence. She would explain or not, when she was ready. I hoped, for her sake, it was just his work, as a lawyer, that kept him away.

Meanwhile, half the residents of the park innocently walked past Marianne's teeming porch and were invited in by the guests already there. Her basic offering of sweet tea, water or beer was supplemented by most everyone who walked in; just the way it was done. Someone brought chips, and they spilled over the middle of the biggest table.

Rose and I were busy. Not particularly social, we were more comfortable coming and going from the kitchen.

I pushed my way through the circle of women around the grill to Pete and the Colonel. I delivered a beer to Pete and bourbon to his helper, as requested.

"New batch ready," announced JJ. Women held out plates with dabs of beans and cornbread, empty buns.

"What would you like?" He asked each politely as he looked down at the coals and fiddled with the grill fork, poking and moving cooked meat around.

"I'll take a little of whatever you want to give me," was the drawled answer. Startled, he looked up into Summer's face as there was a collective, Southern gasp from the other women.

I happened to be looking toward Ronnie and Reggie at the time. They were dressed tastefully, a little upscale for here. She had elegant gel nails that matched her dress, her lipstick and her shoes. It seemed a little pretentious since I had discovered their home in Nashville was for sale and nearly in default. Desiree knew everything, and what she didn't know, Pete did.

Reggie was wearing a button-down shirt, albeit short sleeved. He choked on his hot dog as he laughed at the reaction to Summer. Ronnie glared, but it was lost on him as he coughed and tried to breathe.

As the hussy sauntered away, I saw Betty pat Pete on the arm and ask for a burger. I glanced over at Doris. She was busy talking to Rose Marie as she refilled the tea dispenser.

Summer brushed past motorcycle guy. He hadn't been invited, either. Her arm had touched his as she passed him, but she didn't even look his way. He just looked yearningly after her.

Low voices resumed through-out the porch. I heard Reggie try to soothe his wife. He whispered that it was just like his girl to go after what she wanted. He was proud of her.

The manager, Desiree, had come with a date, a guy with a matching caramel complexion, dreadlocks, and he had large holes in his ears. I couldn't really describe him past those last two characteristics, since that's where my eyes kept going to.

Harold was stag, enjoying the company of whoever was closest to him, but Rose Marie's other regular client, Daniel, had a woman from out of the park somewhere.

Carlotta, the crazy cat lady, was putting hotdogs in her pocket. Carlotta was about a hundred years old; and her over-the-number-limit cats were grandfathered in. She took good care of them all. She had a niece who turned up regularly to help her run errands, personal and pet related.

I knew for a fact that when one of the older residents, Molly, had to move to a nursing home, Rose sneaked Molly's cat onto Carlotta's porch in the middle of the night. He was still there.

Mary Lu Scholl

CHAPTER TEN

TOO CLOSE FOR COMFORT

It sounded like gunfire. The repeated popping noises roused me, but not Ashes. It took a few seconds to register that it was outside. I rolled out of bed in my nightgown and practically fell out of the trailer as I pulled my kitty-gate to, behind the screen door.

By the time I got my bearings and figured out the noise was coming from Ronnie and Reggie's carport, it stopped.

I hurried up the rip-rap drive, swearing about my lack of shoes but refusing to go back after them.

I knew it was probably a vain hope to see someone; no one had seen the Firecracker-Crackpot yet. I was there when Ronnie and Reggie poured out their door. Ronnie glared at me suspiciously.

JJ hurried down his steps across the drive. Catherine flung open her door, but stood unmoving at the top of her ramp, cell phone in hand.

A few others milled around in the street by the time a siren came in from the highway. He turned off the siren but kept his lights on as he turned unerringly down the right street.

Deputy Charlie, it had to be.

"I heard about this from some of the other residents at the party. I don't know why whoever it is picked us, we hardly know anyone." Ronnie was getting up a good head of steam until she realized who the deputy was.

Probably in bigger cities, you would get different officers on different calls. Not here; we pretty much belonged to the same few deputies.

Guilty embarrassment over the domestic scene from the deputy's last visit took the steam out of Ronnie's self-righteous indignation.

Charlie, bless his pea-pickin' little heart, either never noticed her sudden discomfiture or ignored it. "Now Miss Ronnie, I'm sure it was just random; at least that's the conclusion we've come to. Now, have you seen anyone hanging around your place?"

Reggie took over from there. "No, Officer. We haven't noticed anyone, have we, Dear?"

"There was that man who brought *your* daughter home yesterday, on a *motorcycle,* from that *bar* around the corner." Ronnie bit the words out. She really looked terrible in the middle of the night without make-up. The porch light and reflections cast small shadows on her face and arms, accentuated the dark circles under her eyes, lines above them, a scar on her chin and a red mark high on her forehead.

"He's not a stranger. He's Summer's friend. Would you like to talk to him,

Officer?" Reggie seemed immune to his wife's nasty undertones as he put his arm around her. She shrugged him away and tried to smooth her wild hair down over her brow.

"Maybe your daughter can tell me who he is and if she has seen anyone else around. Can you get her while I ask a few of these other folks?" Deputy Charlie opened his notebook and turned to face the crowd. Naturally, I was in front.

"Miss Patty, did you see anyone?"

There being a fat chance of anyone else seeing the guy, since they all turned up after me and *I* didn't see anyone, I very nearly described a leprechaun just for the hell of it.

I couldn't do it. Charlie was a good kid just doing his job. Maybe I was getting soft.

Besides, I didn't have my teeth in. I was lucky I had my glasses on. "No. I'm going back to bed."

I picked my way gingerly over the rough driveway, the rocks sharper when you're not in a tearing hurry. I resisted the temptation to sit on my porch and watch.

Not-so-early the next morning I was making oatmeal, stirring in sweetened, condensed milk, raisins, and diced apples, when there was a knock on my door.

"Eggs?" asked Catherine.

"Nope. Oatmeal with apples, raisins and sweet milk. Want some?"

"Can't be as good as your eggs, but I'll try it."

I made a second bowl and offered her water. We settled on the porch.

"You missed all the excitement last night."

"No I didn't."

"Did too."

I looked sideways at her.

She looked smug.

"I was the first one out there, since it was practically in our backyard."

"That blonde from down south turned up missing."

I had to think about that. Then I remembered that Ronnie and Reggie mentioned a home in Fort Myers, so she must be talking about Summer.

I snorted. "Missing? Some good old boy will be dropping her off in last night's clothes and a hangover this morning."

"Not likely. She's dead."

My jaw dropped open.

Catherine chuckled and I was indignant on the hussy's behalf.

"*That's* not funny; *you* are," She chuckled again. "I beat you to the punch in your own backyard. When Ronnie couldn't find her for the deputy last night, she tried to play it down, but Reggie was obviously upset. He kept asking his wife where Summer was. They nearly got into a shoving match over it."

"That teen-age deputy has good instincts," Catherine added. "He came back this morning and found her in the retention pond."

I couldn't dispute the facts. Disgruntled, I corrected the only thing I could. "He's twenty-four."

This time, Catherine snorted.

Mary Lu Scholl

CHAPTER ELEVEN

Ms. Ricklebauer-Johnson

I had just settled on my porch with my computer and water when my favorite detective pulled into the cul-de-sac.

Detective Danny and I had become acquainted through a number of park problems - mostly murder. I liked his manner, and could also admit he was an attractive man. Blonde-gray hair, built big, and had a nice smile.

There was a twinge of professional jealousy when he stopped in front of Catherine and JJ's. He got out and I saw indecision, which door? He picked the front one and the good Colonel answered. He came out and they settled onto the PVC and glass furniture that had somehow stayed when Albert's trailer left.

I tried to ignore them, and started a new chapter on my next novel, Modular Murder.

After I rewrote the same page the third time, I closed that document and started a letter to the editor about the coming toll road that was going to come up behind the park on its way north. I wasn't really going to mail it, so I just ranted and made up facts to support my arguments as they suited me. It did the trick of taking my mind off Summer and I was almost done with it when a shadow fell over me.

"Good Morning, Miss Patty."

I started to answer and realized I didn't have my teeth in.

"Just a minute," I lisped. Ducking in to get my teeth, I asked him if he wanted water or something. "Root beer kool-aid?"

"Sure. Thank you."

"How do you like our new Pastor?" I asked as I rejoined him. He had lowered himself into the one resin chair I had out beside my glider.

"What's not to like? He seems to be friendly, charming, observant."

I couldn't argue with him there. "Did you meet Catherine?" I was hoping he had missed her and I could give him a hard time.

"She is a very interesting person. She also said to tell you she was sure the only reason I talked to her first was because she was closer, not because she had the presence of mind to record the whole scene on her phone."

She *recorded* it? *Not* my day.

"So what do you need me for?" I griped at him.

He considered me over his jar of kool-aid. "I thought we were friends."

Now I felt guilty. *Definitely* not my day.

"I'm sorry."

He grinned back. "However, that's not why I'm here. I have two reasons to talk to you."

Curiosity got the better of me and distracted me from his tactics.

"I have had your name connected to the firecracker incidents."

Surprise left me speechless; but just for a moment. "You think I'm the Firecracker Crackpot?" I knew my voice squeaked at the end, but I couldn't help it.

He winced.

The department tried to avoid that sort of name for their perps; probably because if one was around long enough to get a name, it highlighted that the department hadn't caught him yet.

"I didn't say *I* thought you were him. However, it begs an answer. Are you?"

"No. Would you expect me to admit it if I was?"

"No. Actually, if it was you and someone asked you, I would expect you to deny it and then never do it again."

I thought quietly, following his premise. "Presuming that if it was me, I was doing it for the notoriety; having accomplished it, I would quit. So, I'd better hope he doesn't stop now."

I looked at him. He just sat there and looked at me.

Now I was irritated. "You know me pretty well. I admit I've been bored, but have you ever known me to do something unlawful?"

He opened his mouth to answer and I had to backtrack quickly. "Unless I was solving a murder. And unless it was necessary."

"Nothing like gunpowder pranks." I grouched.

I could see him evaluating the file he kept in his head with my name on it, and held my breath. I knew he was thinking about stalking, trespass, oh, and breaking and entering...

"No. I think you're impulsive and have boundary issues, but you're not a prankster. The fact remains, however, that you have been seen on the scene at least twice just as they went off; once, hurrying away."

"Boundary issues?" I raised my eyebrows at him.

"Just coincidence," I waved my hand with the pickle jar of kool-aid and nearly spilled it.

He had admitted he didn't believe it was me, and that was all I cared about. I waved my drink again to signal that part of the conversation was over. "Next topic. Summer?"

"Yes. Ms. Ricklebauer-Johnson..."

"Ms. What? No wonder Ronnie didn't introduce themselves with their last name."

"Your neighbors are Johnsons. Ricklebauer was Reggie's ex-wife." He cleared his throat. "Ms. Ricklebauer-Johnson was found this morning lying half-in and half-out of the retention pond. When was the last time you saw the deceased?"

I flashed to the horseshoe pits. "She was having an argument with a guy in a pick-up truck." After seeing her at the party, I knew it had been her. "Wait, that was before the party. I saw her at Marianne's party. She was dropped off by a guy in a black Range Rover."

Detective Danny scrambled to catch up. "A Range Rover, not a pick-up truck?" He flipped the page on his omnipresent notebook.

"No, no. A few days before the party, I saw her meeting someone in the common area. She was having an argument with a guy in a pick-up truck. He was angry about something, and when he saw me he grabbed her and left."

"Abducted her and you didn't call us?"

"No, no. She got in the truck willingly; well, after he insisted." I frowned.

"A black truck?"

"I think it was tan. Well, kinda yellow. You know, that goldish color."

"Not black? You were pretty definite about the black."

"Keep up, Danny. The first time I saw her was with Colonel Saunders in his gold Sebring. The next..."

"Colonel Saunders?"

"Sorry, my fault. JJ next door, he looks like Colonel Saunders. The next time, she was arguing with the guy in the gold-ish, tan-ish, yellow-ish... " I hesitated.

"Champagne?"

"Thank you. The champagne-colored pick-up truck. The last time I saw her, a black Range Rover dropped her off at Marianne's."

After he drew a couple of arrows and then drew a line through something on the previous page, he looked up.

"Was the same man driving both the pick-up and the Range Rover?"

"It was a nice truck, but how many Range Rover drivers would be caught in a pick-up truck?"

"That's a 'no', then?"

"I don't have any idea. I only saw the pick-up guy for a minute, and I couldn't see into the Range Rover - tinted windows, you know." I sipped my root beer.

"I don't suppose you remember anything about the license plates? Stickers on the windows?"

"Frankly, Summer was pretty eye-catching. I doubt anyone really looked at the guys she was with; much less their vehicles."

"Hey, the new park owners are going to install security gates, and I'll bet they'll have cameras."

"Not much help, today, Patty. Did you ever see her on a motorcycle with anyone?"

"Nope. Heard about it though. Did he hit her? I saw your officers looking for something in the grass and the pond; did she drown?"

He shut his notebook. He had one more question but apparently didn't think I would have an answer.

"Did JJ or Catherine ever mention knowing Ms. Ricklebauer-Johnson before they moved here?"

Mary Lu Scholl

CHAPTER TWELVE

On a Leash

If Ashes wanted out so badly, she was going to have to be there on a leash. I buckled the new cat-harness around her. It was like trying to put a sweater on an ice-cream cone. How tight should it be? Fur squished out everywhere. She had more loose skin than I did, and at least eight legs.

She was not happy. I clipped a light leash onto the harness and opened the door.

She did not run for it like she had yesterday, during the escapade that had precipitated this decision. It took a half-hour, but I had finally found her, disoriented and frightened, nearly to the old road.

So today I scooped her up and put her down on my patio, leash attached.

She collapsed at my feet.

I tugged straight up. It was like picking up a wet towel from the middle, except she didn't drip. She puddled. No, she didn't pee. She just turned herself into a little boneless, furry puddle.

I let her back down and decided to wait her out. I sat in the resin chair because it was closest.

She slowly regained her composure and started to move. I was concentrating so hard on willing her to get up and walk that I didn't even hear Nathan and Miss Mouse. I did hear Angie.

Nathan's big, black lab let out a woof and scared poor Ashes out of at least five lives as I dove head first to cover her with my body. Nathan was startled and dropped the leash. Miss Mouse grabbed it, but wasn't strong enough to hold the Lab. She landed on her rear and squeaked.

Pete appeared out of nowhere and nearly ran over Nathan as he parked his front right tire on the leash. Angie's momentum was curtailed abruptly and she fell back on her haunches.

I gathered my poor frightened puddle-cat up and carried her inside. I kept telling her I would never do that again, and for her to remember that it was safer inside.

I could hear Nathan calling that he was sorry but I didn't even answer, just slammed my door shut.

My heartbeat started to slow back to normal. I undid one buckle and Ashes poured out of the harness and disappeared between the nightstand and the bed.

I continued to apologize to my cat.

It was a good thing my neighbors all knew me well enough to not knock on my door for a while.

Hours later, though, someone finally did just that. I flung the door open, and Pete caught it. He and Doris were standing on my porch.

"Sit down." I growled. "I'll get kool-aid."

When I came back out with the jars, I carefully closed the cat gate, though I doubted I would even see Ashes for days. "Thank you." I handed Pete his jar and sat next to Doris on my glider.

"She's okay?"

He was a cat lover. He understood.

I just nodded.

"I told him he couldn't walk her if he couldn't hold her."

It had been long enough, then, that I could be charitable. "Angie's not a bad dog. I pretty much guarantee Ashes is never coming back out. Between getting lost yesterday and scared to death today..."

Doris fidgeted with her drink.

"How well did you know that girl, Summer?"

From Ashes to Summer, quite a segue. Well, both were female.

"I never actually talked to her. I saw her several times. I understand she was a singer."

"She talked to Pete several times."

Pete shifted uncomfortably. "I'm out and around a lot. I fixed a few things for her folks."

"That they haven't paid him for, yet. Not Park stuff." Doris pointed out. "Anyway, he asked her if she was going to sing at the Sunday service and she said she would have to talk to JJ. Then she asked Pete to put in a good word for her."

"Next thing you know, she was in his car."

Mary Lu Scholl

CHAPTER THIRTEEN

Ms. Ricklebauer-Johnson

I typed in Summer Ricklebauer-Johnson and got absolutely zero, nada, zilch. I thought she was an entertainer?

I typed JJ Jarman into Google. Surely a handsome and charismatic preacher of a large church would have articles about him that would show up on-line.

LOCAL PASTOR HEADS STORM RELIEF

JJ Jarman is encouraging not only the members of his congregation at the Heavenly Hope Non-denominational Church, but also members of other churches in the city to contribute to Storm Sanctuaries, a local non-profit dedicated to sheltering the homeless populations following tropical storms.

It went on to describe how it begged, borrowed, or leased vacant spaces for periods of need.

Heavenly Hope Church Collecting Funds

The church is collecting funds for a youth center to be built on unused property that was willed to the church for that use. A benefit is scheduled next Saturday with prominent local entertainers: The Second Chances, The Sunrise Singers, Ushers to Elders, Celestial Seasonals.

There were a few other stories that mentioned him in connection with that same church. The last one was a good-bye supper being held to wish him well on his move north to Citrus County, a couple of months ago.

There was a knock at the door just as my phone beeped at me. I looked at the message display as I growled "Just a minute!"

It was Nick. I didn't even read the text, just tossed the phone onto my bed and flung the door open.

"Good thing I know you and was ready for the door or you'd have knocked me out."

"I'm sorry, Rose. Want to come in or want me to come out?"

"Out."

I handed her a jar of kool-aid as I pulled my screen and the kitty gate closed.

She had a covered plate. "I was taking this to the Johnsons'. I thought they were back from the funeral home, but they disappeared again between my seeing their vehicle and getting the food together. Want some?"

I picked up a corner of the cloth. Two mugs of carrot soup and two big halves of a sausage sandwich. "Do you have to ask?"

She set it on top of the cat crate that doubled as a table and took half. "Anything new on Summer?"

"Et tu?"

"You have to admit, we expect a lot out of you when it comes to this sort of thing."

"Catherine won't admit to knowing Summer before. After Danny asked, I was sure she had probably been a singer at one of JJ's churches or functions or something. I can't get them to connect on the internet. I tried to look at Summer's Facebook page, but if she had one, someone already took it down."

"Even so, they seemed friendly enough." She took a sip of the thick, spicy soup.

"I'm trying to find the guy with the truck or the one with the Range Rover. Trouble is,

I don't run in her circles - whatever circles they were. I've decided to take up drinking. Do you want to go to that bar around the corner with me?"

She almost dropped her sandwich. She caught the falling catsup with cat-like reflexes and her napkin. "When?"

I laughed at her. "Tonight. Do you want to invite Marianne? Or Catherine?"

"I can't believe *I* agreed to go. Give me a minute to absorb this." She shook her head and finished the soup. "How about Marianne?"

On the way over to ask Marianne, we discovered the Johnsons had returned. Rose Marie had more food at home, so we took a shortcut to her house and fixed another plate.

"Won't you come in?" Reggie was at the door before we even knocked. "My wife's gone to lay down." Her face showed briefly in the hallway, a long-sleeved bathrobe and an opaque floral hairnet pulled down over her head; she didn't say a word, just disappeared.

Reggie was the one who looked like he needed to rest. His complexion was pale, the muscles in his face, haggard.

"We just brought some food for you both." Rose's voice was soothing and gentle.

I hovered in her shadow, trying to remember to be circumspect and polite. I could hear Albert scolding me in the past for being single-mindedly abrupt. The social niceties, as Cheyanne used to call them, were just a hindrance to getting information.

While Reggie and Rose passed useless and tired phrases back and forth, I looked around the room. The party offered when they arrived a few weeks ago had never come to pass, so this was the first time I had been in here. At least the first time after the former owner, Jessica...

I heard Reggie say something about a singing group and perked up.

"I have pictures of some of the events she sang at." His voice petered out as he seemed to recognize that Rose was losing interest.

"I'd like to see them."

Rose looked at me in amazement. I was pretty amazed myself. I needed to know more about this girl if I was going to solve this.

The change that came over Reggie's face made the sacrifice of time worth it, even to me. He lit up, his voice was stronger as he led the way into his study.

The rest of the house, the part we had seen, was decorated in the impersonal way that model homes are; carefully matched colors and knick-knacks, regionally appropriate prints on the walls.

The office, though, was all Summer. The little girl with a microphone sparkled and grew up in a myriad display of pictures. In some she was alone, in others with a group. There were awards on the walls and thank you letters from non-profits and churches in between the photos.

In the more recent pictures she was mostly in groups and a little of the shine seemed to be fading. Her hair was looking too young for her face, her make-up a little more prominent. He took one down and offered it to me to look closer. "This was the last group she was with, before..." he bit his lower lip and stopped. I mentally filled in "...she was killed."

There were three women and a man; it was glossy and had one of those automatic dates in the corner some cameras insert. Three years ago. One woman sat with a shiny purple drum-set, another behind a keyboard, and the man had an Ovation. Summer held a mic.

Really? She hadn't entertained for the last three years?

Mary Lu Scholl

CHAPTER FOURTEEN

Research

Marianne was horrified. "You want to go *where?*"

Her astonishment acted as a catalyst to Rose Marie's resolve. "You don't think we know how to comport ourselves in public?"

"You, yes. Patty, no." Shocked at her own response, she covered her mouth with her hand.

"Well, thank you very much!" I put on my best hurt face and left.

Rose caught up with me a minute later. "She's really sorry."

I laughed at her. "Actually, I thought that went better than I expected. Is she coming?"

"Well, no."

"I assume Dan will bail us out if we get into trouble..."

"You, maybe. About Dan..."

"Tell me over a glass of wine or a Dirty Monkey."

Three hours later I drove us to The Hog Wild. I replaced my usual shorts and nurse-scrub-top (pretty, light, comfortable, washes well, has large pockets) with a tie-dye sundress. Rose Marie looked airy and cool in a trendy, floral dress and pretty sandals in place of her crocs.

The good news is that mine was not the only truck. I didn't see the champagne-colored truck, but there was a black Range Rover peeking out from behind the building. There were also a half-dozen motorcycles scattered on the gravel and grass.

Predictably, every eye in the place turned on us when we came in. The only woman in the building seemed to be a buxom brunette behind the bar.

"Do we just sit at a table, or do we have to get our own drinks at the bar?" I whispered, "it's been a while since I did this."

"I think we ought to go up to the bar. We probably want to talk to her anyway."

Bar stools are designed for tall people. It was embarrassing.

"What can I get you ladies?" She smiled with genuine curiosity on her pretty face. Long brown hair was caught up in a bun secured by a pen. Minimal make-up was unexpected, but the tiny tattoos scattered on her shoulders were not.

Rose Marie asked for a glass of white zinfandel.

"Red wine or white wine, that's it. Which one?"

As Rose sipped her white and grimaced slightly, I bravely asked for a Dirty Monkey. The girl laughed and said it was a good thing this wasn't the only bar she'd ever worked in. Then we compromised on a white Russian.

"Did you know Summer?"

"The ditz...I mean, yes. It was a terrible thing."

"Did she talk to you?"

"Nah; wrong sex. She only talked to men. Rex, over there," she pointed, "she sat with him a lot. Seemed to get intense."

"Join you?" Rose asked and smiled.

He glanced up at her and then at me. "Seriously?" He swept his arm in a sideways motion that indicated we could sit.

"Why me? Why today?" He thought better of his question as he held his hand up to forestall an answer. "Aren't you the broad that Pete says interferes with everything, especially the murders we've had since you arrived...? Never had any problems until you got here."

"I don't know you," he declared in Rose's direction.

"I don't get out, much."

"Yes. We're here about Summer."

"I didn't do it; go away."

He continued talking, but without withdrawing his dismissal. It would have been rude to get up and leave while he was talking, was I right?

"She was a nice girl. Talented. I only heard her sing to the jukebox," he nodded toward an ancient one in the corner, "but I know talent when I see it." He frowned. "Hear it." "Heard it."

Apparently this was not his first beer of the evening. "She had bad breaks. All she wanted to do was start over somewhere quiet." He finished the last inch in his glass. "Classy girl like that..." His voice petered out. "The government makes it impossible for anyone to get ahead unless they're already ahead." I could tell he was launching into a conspiracy theory.

Rose asked me with a silent nod if she should get him another beer. I gave her a horrified face at the thought of him riding his motorcycle after another one. She agreed silently. I tried to redirect him. "How was she trying to start over? What was she looking for, here?"

"That's a stupid question. Bourbon. That's what she came here for. Even drank classy...no beer for her." He was obviously focused on the immediate surroundings.

"Anyone else we could talk to?" Rose asked the girl at the bar. Rexy hadn't even noticed we were gone and was still ranting about the government.

"Not right now. The owner, Barry O'Leary, took her home a couple of times to make sure she had a safe ride, but they never talked. Here, anyway," she corrected herself. She wiped down the already glossy, clean bar. The cedar was so shiny it reflected the televised football game behind it.

She seemed to reconsider. "She did ask for him, though, the first time she came in. It seems she came from Fort Myers; so did he, before he bought this place two years ago. So either someone sent her here or she knew who he was and where to find him." She dried her hands. I'll go get him."

"I fail to see why I should tell you anything about Summer. She was my customer here. You are, if you'll excuse the term, a busybody with no place in that girl's sorry drama." Steel glinted in the cold gray eyes that matched his full head of hair.

It was apparent we would get nowhere with him.

At least we knew who drove the Range Rover.

Mary Lu Scholl

CHAPTER FIFTEEN

Complicated Relationships

"I know, Miss Patty. I've already talked to him. Not a very friendly guy, but he genuinely liked Summer and wants us to find her killer. He knew her in Fort Myers. When she wanted to relocate, he suggested here."

"Well, if he truly liked her and it was his fault she was here, he probably feels guilty. That might be why he was so nasty to me."

"Probably. Why else would anyone be mean to you?" He hesitated long enough for me to suspect sarcasm.

"You haven't found the guy in the truck, have you?" Deputy Danny asked, hopefully.

I snorted and hung up. All my call to the Sheriff's Office had accomplished was letting me know my detective hadn't found truck-guy either.

If I was going to go to church, I needed to get dressed. While it wasn't really a church, just the clubhouse, somehow the jeans and tank top most of the attendees wore to watch a televangelist just didn't seem respectful enough for a real, live vicar.

I needed to know more about JJ Jarman. He had befriended Summer immediately; or she, him. Why? Did she just have an innate talent for recognizing people from her hometown?

There were already a dozen people in the room when I arrived. There was an altar cloth over the podium that usually stood in the corner. I thought I recognized Betty's handiwork, there.

A tiny, home karaoke machine stood next to it, hooked up to a laptop. Pete was on his knees next to it, fiddling with wires. Doris was settled at one end of the first row of chairs. They had been set up in rows, with the tables all pushed to one side. I sat one seat over from her, leaving a space for Pete. She lumbered her body up and scooted over, leaving him the aisle seat and making it easier to talk to me.

"How's the case coming?"

"It's complicated. She was a woman who engendered strong emotions. Someone either loved her or hated her. Both emotions can lead to murder."

"Wow. That was deep. Who are you and what did you do with Patty?"

She was probably just teasing, but how could I know that? I don't remember what my excuse was, or if I even made one, but I stood up and walked away just as Marianne walked in.

Marianne moved up to the front row and didn't even notice me. She was singularly focused on the podium and the man studying his Bible on top of it. I hadn't given him a second look, yet.

Colonel Saunders looked very pastoral up there. The wild white hair gave him passion and intelligence. The little beard and mustache gave him sophistication in a way that eluded Deputy Charlie. The Bible was a large tome bound in dark leather. Delicate paper was handled gently with long, careful fingers.

We still had a few minutes so I went out the door for fresh air and solitude. There were about twenty people now. I glanced over at Dahlia's swing. She wasn't there. I searched quickly for her turn-of-the-last century, eight-year-old figure. There was a porch swing on the carport of the same house. She was there, with another figure. I squinted to get a better look just as I heard Colonel Saunders clear his throat and call us to order.

I scooted back in but took a seat at the rear, this time.

He announced a hymn, and the words magically appeared on the karaoke machine. "...provided kindly by Miss Marianne to the park, for use by whoever is providing spiritual service to this community." His gratitude was palpable as he acknowledged Marianne. She lowered her eyes and blushed slightly at the speech.

I hardly heard a word. I hadn't seen any ghost but Dahlia since Albert left. Dahlia was extremely anti-social, but seemed to have a companion this morning. The Patty who had relocated here two years ago would have simply left the service at the whim. Albert, Cheyanne, and Rose Marie had instilled a modicum of social awareness in me. So, the new, socially acceptable, Patty waited impatiently and swore under her breath. When I finally went out, Dahlia and her companion had disappeared. I glanced at the windows to the clubhouse, having seen Dahlia there, just once. No.

I knew Rose Marie was baking, it was Sunday, after all, so I headed over to her house.

I called out as I entered her kitchen. The yeasty smell was heavenly, but the sight was less so. Rose was crying as she kneaded a huge ball of bread dough. When she saw me, she wiped her eyes with the back of her three-quarter length sleeve.

"Good morning, Patty."

I remembered I had cut her off when she tried to tell me about Dan, and then never gave her the time at Hog Wild. "Don't good-morning me. What's wrong?" I snitched a cookie out of her jar - lemon meringue. I took two more.

"Dan. Of course. He doesn't think we ought to see each other anymore. He told his family about me, finally. They object to my being white. Not much I can do about that, is there?"

She covered her bowl and placed it in the warm oven to raise. "How do you fight racism? Why do I feel ridiculous having to when it's normally the other way around. I never dreamed the reason I had never met any of them was because of racism."

My heart melted. "If he chooses his family over you, then he is not worthy. He has sons, right? They're grown. It's really none of their business. Parents? Siblings?"

"You're preaching to the choir, Patty." She gave me a tremulous smile. "He even said the same thing, 'he isn't worthy'. How was church? I can't believe I've seen you in a dress two days in a row! Once to a bar, and then to church! That must tell a story by itself!"

Obviously, Dan was off-limits again.

I gave a brief thought to telling her about Dahlia, but when I had told her about Albert and Cheyanne, it hadn't gone well. Her open-minded attitude didn't readily include ghosts.

"Marianne bought a karaoke machine for singing hymns in the clubhouse." I popped the last carb-free goodness into my mouth. "When did you talk to Dan last?" Maybe I do have boundary issues.

"Yesterday. I made some lame excuse to call. He sounded glad to hear from me. He said he hoped we were still friends." She punched the dough ferociously.

Rose had actually met him in the baking aisle at the market; her lawyer-boyfriend was quite a passable baker. "Should I haunt the grocery store and give him my opinion when he turns up to buy vanilla?"

She actually had to look at me to see if I was kidding. Then she changed the subject. "Summer?"

"I'm sure she sang at the church JJ came from, at least once. I have to keep in mind it was a *very* large church. I'm sure he knew her, I just can't figure out why he won't admit it. Catherine won't, either."

"That's easy. Whatever connection they had in Fort Myers had to be unsavory for some reason. Catherine thinks JJ did it, so she has to protect him."

I just stared at her.

Mary Lu Scholl

CHAPTER SIXTEEN

The Internet, Garbage in, Garbage out

Breakfast was a smoothie made of zucchini bread, cream cheese and buttermilk. Rose Marie had insisted that smoothies were a great breakfast diet drink. My recipes tasted better than hers. They might not be quite so good for me, but they can't be healthy if you don't drink them!

    The Tenant Association Meeting was

later that day, so I needed to go tell Catherine. Things had been a little cool between us since she denied knowing Summer from Fort Myers. For some reason, I was convinced she was not telling the whole truth, and then I got the impression she was avoiding me. After Rose Marie's perspicacious take on it I was even more sure there was more to the story. The fact that Danny had the same feeling, set it in stone.

It occurred to me that I could text the information to Catherine and not have to see her - until whatever drug JJ gave her wore off. I pulled out my phone and realized I hadn't read my son Nick's last text, much less answered him.

Hey Mom. I was telling this woman I

work with about your books. I realized I don't know what name you use when you publish them? I checked under Carlton...

His last name was Carlton. I had twice before gone back to that name between husbands. This time, however, I had stayed with Decker after Don died. It was a lot of effort to change names.

Nick was right, if you don't have the right name, you're invisible on the internet. I texted him back to have her look under Patty Decker.

By the time I had texted him back, I was in front of Catherine's door. *Why, when we weren't getting along?*

Friends don't let friends sleep drugged, that's why.

I went home to get two of Rose Marie's

orange-cranberry muffins.

Catherine's door was slightly ajar. "Come in, just shut the door behind you. I wondered where you went to when I saw you coming but you didn't knock."

I handed her a muffin. "Tenant Association Meeting tonight." I peeled paper off mine and looked around for what to do with it. She reached for it and it disappeared with hers.

"I'll try to stay awake."

"Do you want me to come get you? Or do you want to come to my house for dinner and avoid the whole ingesting-a-downer thing?"

"Okay. What time?"

"Five o'clock." I got up to leave, and turned back at the door. "Allergic to anything?"

"Deputy Detectives."

I was searching again. The trick is to ask the right questions. Nick asking me about my writing name spurred me to wonder what Summer's stage name was. I tried Summer Johnson. I tried Summer Ricklebauer. Surely that was the name she would drop. I wondered what the name of her group was. Then I wondered if they would come to her funeral or memorial service.

Then I realized I hadn't heard anything about a service.

I was standing on Reggie's porch, strange how I always associated the house with him, not Ronnie. There was a big FOR SALE sign in the window. I just stood there stupidly reading the sign without knocking. Ronnie yanked the door open abruptly and nearly ran into me.

She had cut, permed and dyed her hair. She had taken time and a heavy hand with her makeup and it covered the signs of ravaged distress I had seen the last time we had been here.

When we both had recovered from surprise, she snapped at me. "What are you doing here? Don't think I don't know you're poking around in things that don't concern you."

"I came to see if there was going to be a funeral or memorial service and to ask if you need help?"

"Reggie! You have company."

She pushed past me, slammed out the screen porch door (recently repaired) and backed into the road without looking.

I didn't know what to do. That short speech was the total repertoire I could think of. This was not my thing. What was I going to do now? Where was Rose Marie?

Reggie stood in the doorway.

"I'm sorry I upset her. I just wanted to find out if or when a service was planned," I stuttered. Then I wondered if I had insulted him with the 'if' option.

He didn't seem to notice, just turned back into the house. I followed him. wondering if his lack of response was an implied invitation, or if I did have boundary issues.

Spread all over the coffee table were photos. "I was choosing some for the video that will play at the memorial service. I think this one for the hand-out." He handed me one of a sparkling and vivacious thirty-something Summer.

I made some kind of appreciative noise and wished I was anywhere but there. His wife should be helping.

As if he could read my mind, he looked up. "I'm sorry about Ronnie. I don't understand what has gotten into her. She and Summer never got along. Of course Summer was grown by the time I married Ronnie. They did nothing but fight." He took the picture back and set it with a typed page, one scribbled on and edited for the funeral hand-out. "I guess she is regretting their relationship; she has been absolutely beside herself since..."

Reggie seemed to have a penchant for trailing off at the end of his thoughts. He looked so lost and alone that I picked up the picture and paper to give it another sincere look and assure him it was perfect. I looked down in order to be convincing, saw the name at the top and very nearly didn't hear what he said next. The name was Sue Ellen Johnson.

"The service will be in Fort Myers. The Sheriff's Office has given us leave to go down there for a week or ten days. No one here really knew her well, except for JJ," then he added, "and her ex-brother-in-law, Mr. O'Leary."

Mary Lu Scholl

CHAPTER SEVENTEEN

Working together?

My mind was going in different directions as I left the Johnson's.

I saw Catherine making her way down her ramp.

Crap. Dinner.

"Veggie omelet with sweet potato pancakes?"

She had been looking down at her feet

and the ramp. She brought her head up sharply at my voice and nearly toppled off of it.

"Sounds good." She nodded at a covered basket on her patio table. "Dessert."

I'm not sure I would have considered dessert with that menu, but I hadn't run the it past her earlier.

"Cheesecake bites."

I was suddenly considering dessert. "I'll carry it, you'd probably drop it."

She just grinned at me.

Catherine chattered all the way to the Tenant Association meeting. I matched my pace to hers and was counting steps, only half listening.

"..probably won't sit next to you. We need to split up if we're going to clear my JJ of this mess."

This was the first time the subject of JJ and Summer had actually come up between us since I asked if they knew her. I knew it wasn't by accident she was springing this on me only feet from the clubhouse.

I lost track of our steps and that added to my preoccupation and the irritation I had felt earlier..

We parted at the door, and I was back in my earlier funk. People milled around with omnipresent coffee or pop. I was edgy.

Doris fidgeted with her drink. "Did Ronnie kill her step-daughter?"

I swallowed my water wrong and coughed.

She continued, "You know these things."

"What makes you think she did it?" I asked suspiciously.

"Well it was obvious they hated each other. Ronnie was asking us if we knew of an AA group for Summer that was close by."

"Pete says everything they own is for sale. Ronnie said Reggie had practically mortgaged both their souls for that girl the last few years."

"Did she happen to mention why?"

"No. Pete and I have talked about it. Rehab comes to mind."

Pete caught the tail end of it as he walked up. "Still drinking, though, so it didn't take."

He led Doris up to the head table.

I suddenly had no interest in the meeting. There were too many loose ends and I felt like *I* was unraveling instead of the mystery.

I slipped out the door as everyone else was finding a seat.

I glanced down the street to Rose Marie's house. I saw the big black electric bat-mobile parked in front. Indecision slowed my steps.

Then I couldn't stand it. There were so many things I couldn't do. I couldn't help Catherine because I really felt JJ might have had something to do with it. I wanted to help Marianne because I didn't trust JJ. I couldn't prove I wasn't the Firecracker Crackpot. I couldn't help Reggie with his very real grief. It wasn't my place to do so, but his wife was certainly not helping him.

Husbands just die and leave you. My son moved away. My best friends had left me.

I really, really, missed my dog.

Here was something I could do. I could protect Rose Marie. I marched up to Rose Marie's door and banged loudly on the siding as I opened the door.

Rose Marie took one look at my expression and interrupted me before I could say a word. "It's okay, Patty. Come in." In a move that was uncharacteristic of our relationship, she hurried forward and pulled me into a surprised and stiff hug.

Dan was standing behind her and shifting his weight from one side to the other as I glared at him.

"I'm going to marry him, Patty."

He gave me a tentative smile. "She said 'yes' to me."

"Please tell me you'll be my witness." She drew back but still held one of my arms. Did she think I was going to attack him? "Just a small service. You're the only one I want to come. He has a good friend, too. It'll probably just be the four of us."

"Are you sure?" I ignored him and the fact that he was right there. He had her in tears only days ago. There were tears in my eyes, now; damn him. "Are you really sure?"

Perhaps because I saw him holding his breath as he waited with me for her affirmation, I accepted her "yes." I gave her a slightly less-stiff hug and told her I'd be back later.

As I stumbled down the stairs and down the road in a daze, I saw JJ sitting by Marianne through the window of the clubhouse.

I kept going. I had been married four times, why was I suddenly so down on the institution? Why was the idea of Rose Marie and Dan, and Marianne and JJ, putting me in a panic?

I passed Dahlia's swing and it was unaccountably empty. I glanced to the clubhouse and saw Dahlia and a slim blonde woman sitting on a bench.

I marched toward them. I wanted to talk to that woman. Dahlia actually raised her hand to wave at me. The woman glanced at her, then at me, and disappeared. Dahlia looked startled, then shrugged and disappeared too.

Mary Lu Scholl

CHAPTER EIGHTEEN

It was Just All Piling Up On Me

I was exhausted by the time I made it back to my trailer. I turned my phone off. I considered firing up the computer and following up on all I had learned today. Instead, I sat on my bed and leaned against the curved wall on the far side. I slid down the wall over the next few minutes. I didn't cry, but my stomach clenched and my chest hurt.

Ashes jumped up and paced around me, meowing softly. Then she curled up under my chin and rested her head on my shoulder. It helped. How do animals know?

CHAPTER NINETEEN

Also Known As...

I woke with a stiff neck, but didn't mind. I stayed in bed a little longer and listened to my cat purr. The discomfort of my twisted clothing finally led me to gently move her and mix a glass of my latest MIO Energy flavor, cherry.

I finally felt human again after I put on clean clothes. I reached for my phone.

There were messages from last night and this morning.

"There was another firecracker incident, this time at Pete's during the meeting. Are you okay? We noticed you left."

From anyone but Doris, that would sound like an accusation. I'd call her back in a while.

"Patty. Please call me. I could tell you were upset. It really is okay. I am so happy. You're probably at that meeting, but you'll get this when you get home. Come over for breakfast. Please be happy for us."

I might take Rose up on that. She had all night to think about it. If she hadn't changed her mind by this morning, I could put on my happy face for her sake. Funny. I really liked Dan until he made her cry.

Rose didn't answer her phone. "It's okay; I'm not going to start anything or give you a hard time. I'll see you later in the day since you didn't answer. Don't worry, be happy." On that rather dated, musical sentiment, I hung up and started my own breakfast.

I made my list for the day. I wanted to see Pete and ask him about the firecrackers, and about the meeting. If I couldn't find him I would have to settle for Catherine or Doris. I needed to see Rose Marie. I needed to find out more about Sue Ellen Johnson.

Sue Ellen Johnson. There 497 of them in the United States. Predictably, most in the south. Narrowed to Florida and then to Fort

Myers, I started to look at each one.

One was 97.

One was 6.

The next one was a felon.

Sue Ellen Johnson, a local gospel singer with the Celestial Seasonals, was convicted today of embezzlement regarding the Heavenly Hope Church youth fund.

It was dated a little more than two years ago.

There are mixed emotions regarding the three year sentence because of the notoriety of the crime. The law, however is for the offense and does not increase the penalties simply because the victim, the Church Youth Group, is popular.

The Pastor of the Church spoke eloquently to the judge and the courtroom about forgiveness and blamed the addiction to alcohol rather than Ms. Johnson. In addition to the sentence, which could potentially be reduced for good behavior, she is directed to complete a rehabilitation program, off-site and at her own expense.

Perhaps in deference to the notoriety of the offense, restitution of the $5,000 stolen is required, with court costs, and an additional fine of $10,000 has also been levied.

No wonder Summer was on Ronnie's less-than-popular-step-daughter list!

Mary Lu Scholl

CHAPTER TWENTY

BLACKMAIL?

Rose was a whole different woman from the one I had caught crying in her bread dough.

"Friday."

"I don't have to wear a funny dress in an obnoxious color, do I?"

She laughed. Nothing was going to offend her today. "You can wear whatever you want. You're my best friend."

"You're not going to let JJ officiate, are you?"

"No, no. I don't hardly even know him - except for Marianne's party."

"What has she said?"

"I haven't actually told her, yet. I'm not going to tell anyone until afterward."

"Is that because you don't trust him? If he jilts you I'll poison him painfully - I've made a study of it, you know."

"No, no. I just don't want to deal with the details of a major life change until I have to. You won't put any pressure on me..." Rose stopped to give me a doubtful eye. "Daniel, Howard, Marianne, even Desiree, are going to be full of questions and wanting decisions. I'd rather just be happy for the moment and worry later."

It had been on the tip of my tongue to ask about her home and her cats. Damn.

Over half of a grilled cheese sandwich, she brought up Summer.

I volunteered my new findings. "You were probably right about Catherine and the Colonel. It turns out Summer was a felon. The reason she's been off the radar and needed a place to "start over" as Mr. O'Leary and Rex mentioned was because she's been in prison for embezzlement. I'd say that was the unsavory connection between her and JJ. I wonder if he was involved, or at least knew ahead of time, about her little scam?"

"Blackmail." Rose nodded, chewing thoughtfully, her suspicions confirmed.

"Blackmail? Not a chance." Catherine snorted. "JJ might have known about it before hand, even tried to talk her out of it, but he doesn't have any money."

"So you would have to pay it."

Startled, she stared at me. "You really think I could have done it? I couldn't have gotten my walker over to the pond even if I had a chance of overcoming her." She shook her head. "You're smarter than that."

"JJ could have, rather than have to ask you for the money."

Did she hesitate?

"Summer wasn't a bad girl, despite appearances to the contrary."

"So we're through claiming not to know her?"

"I knew her. When she wasn't drinking,

she was fun, charming and talented. I liked her at first. JJ just should have been more careful with his bookkeeping, and choice of bookkeeper. Do you want some cookies?"

"Sure. I'll get them. Water?"

I set the plate down between us on her porch. "I knew you knew her. I asked you about her and you said she didn't play an instrument. You also said JJ had been secretive about her; so how would you know?"

"Good catch."

Did I see a hint of respect? Or was it disgust with herself for her incautious statement?

"I really think the embezzlement was more her husband's idea than hers. He was a spiky haired bastard more in love with himself as her *manager*, than with her. She divorced him but wouldn't testify against him."

She dropped peanut-butter crumbs in her lap and stopped to brush them away. "I heard he fought the divorce."

I waited to see if she would hang JJ a little farther out to dry. She stared off across the road toward the retention pond.

Was Catherine remembering what happened? Was she wondering if JJ was, indeed trying to stay out of trouble with her?

For myself, I wondered about her characterization of the Reggie's daughter. Was she just a spoiled child caught up between charismatic men? Was she devious enough to know she could blackmail either JJ or her ex-husband or both?

A lightning bolt hit. The guy in the truck was her ex-husband.

After a few minutes of surprisingly comfortable silence, I gave in first. "Did you know about the firecrackers at Pete's?"

"Pete *is* a firecracker."

Mary Lu Scholl

CHAPTER TWENTY-ONE

Who knew what, when?

"Danny? I'm assuming you know about *Sue Ellen Johnson's* arrest record. I consider it patently unfair you would hold even her real name back on me." I was working up a head of steam as I headed over to Pete's. I nearly tripped as I tried to snarl into the phone and walk at the same time.

I stopped and plopped down onto a bench. Across from me, Dahlia and, I presume, Summer, sat on a porch swing.

I glared at the silent, attractive specter.

Detective Boatright made conciliatory noises that I didn't even listen to. I interrupted him.

"Have you found her sneaky ex-husband, yet? Not only could she have been trying to blackmail JJ, but I don't really think so; she could also have been blackmailing her ex."

The blonde ghost scowled at me.

"How would I know what her ex's name is? Something O'Leary."

The voice I had considered to belong to a friend launched another attack. "Where were you when the firecrackers went off under Pete's golf cart?"

Speechless, I held the phone away from me and stared at the screen. I thought we had dealt with that. Then I thought back. Where had I been?

I had ducked out of the Tenant meeting, something I never missed.

The voice on the other end said something, but I couldn't understand him, the phone was too far away and not on speaker.

"I was home asleep." I sadly hung up on him.

I sat there a very long time, not really seeing anything going on around me.

I wondered if Pete had thrown me under the bus for not being at the meeting. With less anger, and more sadness, I continued on to his house.

Pete was on the phone but waved me in. "Ralph has security cameras, and one is pointed at my carport. If he still has them running I might be able to catch the Firecracker Crackpot."

"So you didn't tell your brother-in-law that it was me, since I wasn't at the meeting?"

"Why, no! Why would I do that? Why would *you* do that? That's absurd."

He started to put his phone down. "You didn't, did you?"

"Of course not." I gestured toward his phone that was ringing almost silently. He put it on speaker and set it on his desk. He booted up his computer.

"Hey, Pete. What's up?" Ralph's voice boomed through the air.

"Shouldn't you be back on your way down here?"

"Thinking about it. The wife has a few things she needs to see to. Probably closer to the end of the month."

I fidgeted through their polite discourse. *Enough already* was on the tip of my tongue.

Pete grinned at me. He knew I was impatient and would consider this polite chit-chat as inane.

"Do your security cameras still work?"

"Sure they do."

"I mean, are they running?"

"As far as I know. I haven't checked on them for quite a while."

"I need to look at the feeds for the last few days. Can I use your key and go in and check them? Do I need a password?"

"You can do it from your own computer. Let me get the access and password for you, I went wireless last winter. What's happened, by the way?"

We could hear drawers opening and papers shuffling.

"Just someone setting off firecrackers, and I can see one of your cameras aimed at my carport."

"Nothing wrong at my place, right? I heard about the firecrackers. Doris told my wife a while back. Here it is. It's backed up to the cloud, so you should be able to go back quite a while."

He read off numbers and letters and gave Pete instructions that just bounced around in my head like BBs in a boxcar.

I snapped back to the present when Pete

suddenly had eight rectangles dividing up his monitor. He was scrolling them back in time to catch the Firecracker Crackpot when I noticed that one of the cameras was aimed at the retention pond.

I grabbed his arm. "Can this go back to the night Summer died?"

"Mmmm. We'll have to look. Let me find the firecracker person first, it's closer."

"Pete? Can you help me bring in the groceries I bought you?" Doris was at the door.

""Yeah, hang on. Keep scrolling, will ya, Patty."

No sooner had he turned around than I grabbed the mouse and moved the scroll bar way back and went back too far. Then I waited, nudged the cursor forward, cussed under my breath, and finally got to the night Summer died. I found the double triangle fast forward and found Summer carrying a bottle of what was apparently bourbon picking her way across the grass toward a picnic bench just on the edge of the pond. The security light gave an air of sadness and mystery to .the scene Immediately behind her came Ronnie. Ronnie was gesticulating wildly.

Doris appeared behind me and looked over my shoulder. "Hey..."

"Shush."

Grabbing Summer's arm. Ronnie yanked her around to face her. Summer swung the bottle high and caught Ronnie a glancing blow high on her forehead. She fell, but pulled Summer down with her. Once down,

Ronnie scrambled up to her knees and hit Summer on the head with what looked like her phone. Back on her feet, and Summer still motionless on the bank of the pond, Ronnie aimed a vicious kick at her stepdaughter's back and stalked away.

Doris had been holding her breath, and let it out. "So Ronnie..."

Just then, Summer sat up. She maneuvered her way to the bench and sat there with her bottle. She upended it and then glared at the bottle. In a fit of temper she tried to fling it away, an inebriated, grandiose gesture. It went a about a yard, but the movement messed with her equilibrium and the momentum carried her off the bench. She tried to get back up, but the ground was too steep for her compromised balance and she fell forward into the water.

Pete was back, silent. I left Doris to explain it to him.

CHAPTER TWENTY-TWO

Not exactly viral, bacterial?

I walked across the grass toward my house, but stopped at the bench where Summer had been sitting and drinking. I pulled out my phone after I sat down.

Walking and using my phone was never a good plan for me.

Detective Danny didn't answer his phone; which was fine with me. I wasn't sure I wanted to actually talk to him, anyway.

I *still* didn't know who the FirecrackerCrackpot was. The doubt in the Detective's voice still stung.

Why should I care? He didn't need me and I certainly didn't need him.

Even as I had those rebellious thoughts, I was texting him.

"Call Pete and ask him for his video, he should have figured out how to copy it by now. Don't bother calling me back."

Clouds were rolling in for an evening storm. It would be dark in a few minutes, and I would be wet.

My phone signaled a message, then another one. Pete had sent me two videos. I opened the longer one and found the clip of Summer and her stepmom. I closed it and opened the second one.

The only light was a security light a half block away, and was blocked by a small pine tree that had grown up. A medium height, medium build figure at the very edge of the screen and in the shadows, tossed the firecrackers down the driveway, pulled them back - presumably by the fuse - when they didn't go far enough, and tossed them again. There was a spark and the figure was long gone before it reached the fire-crackers.

I opened the other video again and thought about Summer. Perhaps not particularly bright, but talented. Had I read her wrong? I suddenly wanted to know her better. I raised my voice, "Sue Ellen? Summer?"

At just that moment, Ronnie came charging out of her porch door. I expected to see Reggie come out after her. She started toward her car but saw me watching her from where she had last seen Summer.

Like an angry bear she charged across the road and down the slope.

"It was an accident I tell you! Why did you and Pete have to send that to Reggie? Why couldn't you leave well enough alone? She only brought trouble to her father!"

She didn't even slow up. When I realized she meant to do more than just yell, I started to get up. Like a freight train she struck me dead center. I was bigger, but she had momentum on her side. We both tumbled to the ground. She was still cussing at me and at Summer. "He's going to leave me because of her and she's not even here anymore." She had hold of my hair and was trying to push my head under water. I got one good blow to the side of her head and we both slid farther down the wet grass bank, now fully half in the water and weeds.

"I didn't mean to, but I was GLAD. GLAD do you hear me?"

A pair of strong arms suddenly picked her up and dropped her a few feet away.

"Are you okay?" The gruff voice penetrated the ringing in my ears.

A golf cart slid to a precarious stop sideways on the bank, the higher two tires lifting a second as it nearly toppled. Pete floored it, turning the wheel to the right to keep it from tipping over. Doris was still fifty yards away in her own cart, but was closing fast.

Detective Danny was trying to wrestle the alligator in pastels while trying at the same time to see if I was okay.

I stood up gingerly and painfully. It had all been so unexpected. It was so sad and so unnecessary. She obviously still thought she had killed Summer, had thought so all along. Did she not watch to the end of the video? I wiped the sand and mud from my arms, leaving streaks behind. I just headed blindly for home.

I heard Danny tell someone to "Just let her go."

I stumbled to my door and looked down at myself. I got my shower bag, a quick change and a towel and headed for the shower room. I looked to see if anyone was watching and kept to the shadows as I walked.

The hot water both burned and soothed me as it carried away the panic, the mud and my tears.

I rested my head against the tile.

I had to pull it together.

I had a wedding tomorrow.

For a preview of Modular Murder →

MODULAR MURDER

Just as I turned the key, I heard a shriek. I dropped the keys, *and* my drink. At least the keys were retrievable. My pumpkin drink just puddled at my feet.

It had come from Marianne's. Since when did she get up this early? I hurried over to her door.

She was standing in her living room with her arms crossed over her nightgown. *HOW did she manage to have her hair look so neat just out of bed? I'm lucky if I comb mine before I leave the house.* I ran a hand through my medium length gray hair.

"Are you okay? What's the matter?"

My eyes tracked to where she was looking.

There was a man sprawled on her pink and light blue patterned love seat, facing the television with a beer in his hand. He was putting his naked foot on the floor and drawing the too-small bathrobe across his hirsute chest and saggy lap as he tried to explain.

"...had the television down low so I wouldn't disturb..."

He was cut off by Miss Charles running out of her room. "Teddy, I told you to stay in the room until I could introduce you to Marianne! I hadn't even posted on Facebook that you were here!"

Marianne was almost catatonic at coming out of her room and finding a near-naked man on her couch.

"He...belongs to you, Suzy?"

I scooted across the room to Marianne. I didn't know whether to pat her arm, hug her, or speak, so I just let my presence next to her indicate that I was on her side. It occurred to me I might have to speak, so I checked automatically for my teeth. I was getting better about remembering them. But who worries about being socially acceptable at this hour of the morning – when feeding animals?

"Hair of the dog, you know?" The man with the pillow physique and lots of shaggy hair waved his beer at Marianne and me. "I felt awful and needed a beer."

"Come back to bed, Love. We can sort all this out at a decent hour."

Teddy obediently rose and shuffled after

Miss Charles (Suzy?) into what was apparently, now, *their* room.

Please consider leaving me a review on Amazon or on Goodreads. Reviews are our lifeblood as authors!

Find me at:
https://www.amazon.com/author/maryluscholl

ABOUT THE AUTHOR

Mary Lu Scholl kissed the Blarney Stone and has never looked back.
Retired and living in the paradise of West Central Florida, on the Nature Coast, she writes cozy mysteries for both men and women. She lives with her mom and a cat, around the corner from her daughter. Family is steadily migrating toward the warm climate and she looks forward to having everyone close.

**TRAILER PARK TRAVAILS
PATTY DECKER COZY MYSTERIES**

Camper Catastrophe (Book 1)

www.amazon.com/dp/B07MHV48PH

Mobile Mayhem (Book 2)

www.amazon.com/dp/B07MWBL8P

Birds, Bees and RVs (Book 3)

www.amazon.com/dp/B07PM8Z35H

Trailer Trauma (Book 4)

www.amazon.com/dp/B07YCSS9GS

Modular Murder (Book 5)

www.amazon.com/dp/B084T817MG

Corpse in the Clubhouse (Book 6)

www.amazon.com/dp/B08NJ6B2WF

Restless Retirement (Book 7)

www.amazon.com/dp/B093FWNRGY

Motorhome Motives (Book 8)

www.amazon.com/dp/B09CP1FF29

Fatal Philandering (Book 9)

www.amazon.com/dp/B0C47HRXQ6

Dirt, Drugs and Disaster (Book 10)

www.amazon.com/dp/B0D2SGL6TB

Eventually, Patty encounters Bernie Murphy.
Bernie lives nearby and that's where Nature Coast Calamities pick up.
With a hint of Irish Folklore,

NATURE COAST CALAMITIES

BERNIE MURPHY COZY MYSTERIES

Lecanto Leprechaun (Book 1)

www.amazon.com/dp/B09ZKNVL49

Big Foot and the Bentley (Book 2)

www.amazon.com/dp/B0B7QHJKM2

InverNessie (Book 3)

www.amazon.com/dp/B0BCHCSX3B

Pu'ka and the Pirates (Book 4)

www.amazon.com/dp/B0CGBMVHHT

Made in United States
North Haven, CT
27 March 2025